'There was an enormous, jolting, bone-shaking PHUMPH . . .

Then there was a pause as the sea drew breath.

Then it came again . . . PHUMPH.

The *Crooked Crab* was shaken from bow to stern. Like peas from a pea-shooter, the crew were hurled forward.'

There are all sorts of unexpected excitements for the crew of the *Crooked Crab* when Captain McCorkell goes off on holiday, leaving Bill Brighty in charge. For Bill might have been all right as a mate but he is hopeless as a captain . . .

BY MYSELF books are specially selected to be suitable for beginner readers. Other BY MYSELF books available from Young Corgi Books include:

T.R. BEAR Series by Terrance Dicks
  ENTER T.R.
  T.R. GOES TO SCHOOL
  T.R.'S DAY OUT
MIDNIGHT PIRATE by Diana Hendry
URSULA CAMPING by Sheila Lavelle
THE HAUNTING OF HEMLOCK HALL by Lance Salway
MY GANG by Catherine Sefton
THE KILLER TADPOLE by Jacqueline Wilson

The Tale Of The Crooked Crab

Delia Huddy

Illustrated by Linda Birch

YOUNG CORGI BOOKS

THE TALE OF THE CROOKED CRAB

A YOUNG CORGI BOOK 0 552 524425

Originally published in Great Britain in 1981 by
Julia MacRae Books

PRINTING HISTORY
Young Corgi edition published 1987

This book is set in 14/18 pt Century Schoolbook
by Colset Private Limited, Singapore.

Young Corgi Books are published by Transworld
Publishers Ltd., 61—63 Uxbridge Road, Ealing,
London W5 5SA, in Australia by Transworld
Publishers (Australia) Pty. Ltd., 15—23 Helles
Avenue, Moorebank, NSW 2170, and in New Zealand
by Transworld Publishers (N.Z.) Ltd., Cnr. Moselle
and Waipareira Avenues, Henderson, Auckland.

Made and printed in Great Britain by
The Guernsey Press Co. Ltd., Guernsey, Channel Islands.

The Tale Of The Crooked Crab

Chapter 1

A rusty funnel and a smudge of
smoke, four portholes on one side
and three on the other. A leaning
mast and a patched and faded sail.
That was the *Crooked Crab*.

Captain McCorkell sailed in her
with his crew of five. Five of the

laziest, greediest, most grumbling
ragamuffins that ever sailed the
Seven Seas.

But the Captain, who like a needle
had only one eye, stood no nonsense
from the crew. He made them polish
the brass and stitch the sail and
swab the decks, so that they had no

time to think of other things they would rather be doing.

The *Crooked Crab* was a jack of all trades, a bit of a tramp and a bit of a fishing boat. Sometimes they loaded her hold with a cargo of barley and sometimes they fished for herring.

Until one particular day . . .

On that day the sky was so blue it ran into the sea and the sun hung over the *Crooked Crab* like a juicy orange. Captain McCorkell's thoughts turned to warm yellow sands and little frills of waves breaking on the beach. And counting backwards on his fingers very fast he said, 'I've been Captain of the *Crooked Crab* for fifteen years and never had a single day's holiday.'

So he packed his bag with his bathing costume and his lilo and his hot water bottle (in case the nights turned cold) and he got into the rowing tub and told the mate, Bill Brighty, to row him to a nearby island. There, he said, he would catch a passing boat and go off to some nice seaside town that had a

pier and a band and fish and chips
for tea and lights on the prom in the
evening. He'd have a real rest from
being a captain on the high seas.

He would be away, he said, for
two whole weeks. After two weeks,
they were to pick him up again in
the rowing tub.

But before he went, he told the
crew that he left Bill Brighty in

charge and that each one of them must do exactly as the mate said.

They lined up along the side of the *Crooked Crab* to see the Captain off; Bracken and Uncle Will, Marty Thinface and Potter the Cook.

And when he came to wave goodbye, Captain McCorkell felt really quite sorry to leave them all behind.

Chapter 2

Now Bill Brighty might be all right as a mate but he was no good at all as a captain. Bill Brighty always said "yes". When Captain McCorkell gave orders, Bill Brighty said "yes" at once. This was such a lovely change from the rest of the crew that the Captain made him the mate.

But, when it came to giving orders himself, Bill Brighty couldn't think of any. What's more, people laughed when they looked at him. Poor Bill Brighty was all nose. When he had a cold (which was most of the time) he looked terrible.

For one whole day after the Captain left, things went on as usual. Of course the crew grumbled. Of course Bracken overslept. Marty got stung by a wasp. And Uncle Will, who couldn't swim, fell over the side and had to be rescued in a bucket.

But on Monday trouble began

with Potter the Cook.

'Chocolate mousse?' said Bill Brighty at lunch time (only it sounded like chogolade bousse when he said it). 'Haven't we had rather a lot of chocolate mousse since the Captain left?'

'Crew want chocolate mousse,' said Potter. 'What's more *I* want chocolate mousse. Chocolate mousse is easy to make.'

Potter the Cook made chocolate mousse from a packet. He had packets and packets piled up in the galley.

'Tomorrow we have lamb chops and cabbage,' said Bill Brighty (and that must have been the first order he had ever given), 'or the crew will all get spots.'

'*Fry me aunty*,' said Potter the Cook. 'We shall have what I make.'

And the next day he made chocolate mousse again.

Potter the Cook had started the rot.

Marty Thinface refused to scrub the deck. He fancied sunbathing on it rather than scrubbing it and he said so.

'Scrub the deck or else . . .' said

Bill Brighty trying hard to make his poor blocked-up head think fast.

'Or else what?' asked Bracken.

'Get lost mate,' said Marty Thinface to Bill Brighty.

Getting lost sounded to the mate like going too far. It almost sounded like mutiny. Was it mutiny, he wondered.

'Mutiny?' asked Bill Brighty aloud—most unwisely.

'Mutiny!' shouted Bracken, throwing a scrubbing brush high in the air and missing it as it came down. It bounced on the roof of the deck-house, so that Potter the Cook leaped up from the galley, thinking the *Crooked Crab* was under attack.

'An attack?' asked Potter eagerly.

'Mutiny!' Bracken told him.

'*Fry me aunty*, mutiny!' shouted Potter the Cook in delight.

'Brighty for the plank,' cried Marty, mean and thin.

They seized poor Bill Brighty, bound his hands together behind his back and put a blindfold over his eyes. Then they looked round for a plank.

There were no loose planks on the *Crooked Crab* so they had to take a leaf out of the table in the cabin and use that.

Bill Brighty made no fuss; trussed up like a chicken, he couldn't. Laughed at by the crew, he wouldn't anyway. He had his pride. And it was better to save his breath for swimming to land—for he had no idea how far away that might be.

They pushed him over the side of the ship and he skidded and tottered down the plank.

He fell into the sea before he even reached the end.

And they all went off in the *Crooked Crab* without so much as a

backward glance to see how Bill
Brighty fared.

Chapter 3

The rust crept further up the funnel and the portholes became ringed with green mould. The crew tripped over the ropes that wriggled and snaked across the deck, but never thought of picking them up and coiling them neatly away.

Luckily the weather stayed calm. They didn't bother to start the engine. The sail flapped lazily and the sea lifted the *Crooked Crab* out of the hollow of one wave and dropped her gently into the next.

For the most part the roistering, foistering sailors sat in the cabin with their feet on the table and ate chocolate mousse and drank grog

from the barrels in the hold that Captain McCorkell kept strictly for special occasions.

They went to bed later and later each night and got up later in the morning until one day ran into another and they weren't at all sure whether it was the next afternoon or the morning before.

Nor did they much care.

Potter the Cook said, '*Fry me aunty*; if they do nothing, why should I?' And from that day forward he refused to wash up a single plate, so that the dirty plates were stacked in piles round the cabin and, after they ran out of clean ones, they ate out of saucepans in the middle of the table and dipped their fingers in the chocolate mousse and licked them clean.

It was all very disgraceful and Captain McCorkell would have eaten his captain's hat in horror if he had seen them.

But he didn't.

From time to time, Bracken picked up his mouth organ and played a tune—very patchily—and

they all joined in with growling,
uneven voices, singing,

and other such tuneless drivel.
But everyone can have too much
of a good thing—even lazy
sailors—and after a week of doing
exactly as they pleased, the crew

began to quarrel.

'You're no good,' said Marty
Thinface to Uncle Will—they were
playing noughts and crosses in the
dust on the floor of the cabin—
'You're useless. And what's more
you're a cheat.'

Uncle Will was cross-eyed. He
couldn't see if the noughts were in a
row let alone the crosses. He had
once had a pair of spectacles but he
had lost them years before in a
storm at sea.

'*Useless*,' said Marty again and
gave Uncle Will a sharp dig in the
ribs. But, however useless Uncle
Will might be at noughts and
crosses, he didn't like Marty
Thinface telling him so. He gave

Marty a kick on the shin.

Now Bracken had gone to sleep with his head very close to the game on the floor and Uncle Will's kick caught him a glancing blow on his ear. Only half awake, he punched Marty.

Marty lashed out at Uncle Will *and* Bracken.

Potter the Cook, who never missed the chance of a fight, had joined in before you could say *"Fry me aunty*" and within two seconds everyone was tumbling about and getting tangled up like sheets at the launderette.

And then the worst happened.

Chapter 4

There was an enormous, jolting,
bone-shaking PHUMPH . . .

Then there was a pause as the sea
drew breath.

Then it came again . . . PHUMPH.

The *Crooked Crab* was shaken
from bow to stern. Like peas from a

pea-shooter, the crew were hurled
forward.

For a long moment everyone lay
stunned.

It came a third time.

P H U M P H . . .

And now it was followed by a
slow, creaking, yawning . . .
'E.oow.g.hh.'

The mast, that had never stood

upright anyway, fell onto the deck
with a tremendous crash.

Potter the Cook was first on his
feet—and then Marty Thinface.
They staggered up the stairway and
onto the deck.

A huge shape towered over the
Crooked Crab and, even as they
looked, the swell of the sea lifted
their ship forward and PHUMPH!
there came the fourth collision.

Now on the deck of the *Crooked
Crab* was an old brass cannon. It
belonged to Captain McCorkell. He
took great care to keep it ready and
loaded in case they met an
unfriendly fisherman.

To Potter, the great shadow above
them was more than unfriendly—it

was threatening.

'To the gun,' he shouted excitedly. 'Attack! Let 'em have it boys. Fire the cannon . . .' And even as he shouted, Potter was stumbling over the mess of ropes and the fallen mast, grasping and throttling the gun in an effort to turn it onto their attacker.

Together, he and Marty swung it round and upwards so that the nose

of the cannon was pointing high
above their heads.

B O O M ! ! ! !

There was a roar and a spurt of
flame and a cannon ball streaked
out and away—

'Again!' roared Potter, loading
swiftly. A second cannon ball
followed the first.

Now if only Potter had not been
so hasty, he would have seen

that—far from being attacked by a warship a hundred times bigger than themselves—the *Crooked Crab* had bumped into an oil rig.

The crew of the *Crooked Crab* felt the bump. The men on the oil rig heard it. Half a dozen heads peered over the rail to see what had crashed into them.

When Potter fired the cannon, the shot nearly shaved off one of their beards.

'Hey-ey-ey,' shouted the man on the oil rig angrily. 'Big deal! Mind what you're doing, can't you . . . or we'll give you a dose of the old one two . . .' and then he whipped back his head only just in time as the second shot from the *Crooked Crab* followed the first.

At this second shot, the men on the oil rig were really angry. There was now quite a row of them and they looked down carefully at the *Crooked Crab*, way below, where the whole crew rushed round on the deck like flies that had lost their wits.

They didn't stop to hear the angry shouts from above but went on firing the cannon more and more wildly.

'Like that is it!' said the men on the oil rig in disgust. And seeing that they couldn't hope to make themselves heard above the noise

and the smoke, they went into a
shed and got a barrel of oil.

'Take that, you scum!' they
shouted, 'Skunks . . . *pirates*!' and
they poured the oil over the side of
the rig.

And having emptied one barrel,
they got another and did the same
again. *Glug. Glug.*

The oil landed with a splat on the
deck of the *Crooked Crab*.

It slid down the funnel into the
engine room.

It ran down the stairway into the
cabin where it coated the piles of
broken plates which had fallen all
over the place at the first
PHUMPH.

It got everywhere.

One more barrelful and the
Crooked Crab would have come to
an oily end.

As it was she had a bit of luck.
The waves that had been tossing her
against the oil rig took her right
past and beyond. And very quickly
the ship was out of reach of the
barrels of oil and the angry men on
the rig.

And while the crew skated and
skidded and landed on their backs

on the deck, scrambled to their feet only to fall down again on their knees, the ship was carried away by a most timely current.

No longer a *Crooked Crab* but a crippled one. She had a hole in her side. And because there was no mast to hold the sail, nor a hand on the wheel, the ship went slowly round in circles.

The dipping rays of the sun caught her oily deck. The whole ship turned yellow, orange, red, green, blue, indigo and violet. The *Crooked Crab* became a rainbow-coloured dancer, bobbing and nodding and slowly sinking lower and lower in the water.

Chapter 5

When Bill Brighty walked the plank
and sank like a stone into the sea, he
thought it was the end. But he came
up again, spluttering and snortling,
and found that he could undo his
bonds quite easily for the crew of
the *Crooked Crab* never made a

good job of anything.

Now one thing Bill Brighty could do was swim. After he had shaken the water out of his eyes and coughed the water out of his lungs and sneezed the water out of his nose, he looked up to find the *Crooked Crab* was moving so slowly he could easily catch up with her. So he swam along and climbed into the tub which was tied on behind. Then he undid the towing rope and,

taking the oars out from under the seat, rowed quickly away. And not one of the crew looked back to see what he was doing.

Bill Brighty thought he would row to the island where he had landed Captain McCorkell. He knew of no other land he could make for.

Captain McCorkell was not enjoying his holiday one little bit. It was a very small island with only a cow or two, a few sheep, a farm and a village store. There was no hotel and only one house which had a notice in the window . . .

'VISITORS TAKEN,' read Captain McCorkell, standing outside the house and reading the notice. 'Not even Visitors *Welcome*.'

But it was the only place where he
could stay.

So he had no pier and no
promenade, no band nor bright
lights and—hardly surprising—no
other visitors to talk to. What was
worse, his landlady cooked the most
dreadfully soggy chips.

And as the ship that called at the
island once a month had called there
only the week before, he had no

hope of going anywhere else.

Even the sun, which was shining warmly on the *Crooked Crab* out at sea, was not nearly as warm on this windy island. But as Captain McCorkell was on holiday, he had to bathe each day. Afterwards he sat in a deck-chair on the beach, well wrapped up in a travelling rug and hugging his hot water bottle.

Although the wind might bite, the fish did not. The Captain spent a whole day with a rod and line and caught nothing—except a small muddy shrimp which swam in when his pail fell over in a rock pool.

'Push off,' said the Captain angrily and threw the shrimp back into the sea.

So that when he saw a dot on the horizon which came nearer and nearer and finally turned out to be Bill Brighty in the tub from the *Crooked Crab*, he was delighted.

He wasn't so delighted when he heard Bill's tale of woe.

He said, 'Well you really have messed things up, Bill Brighty. But they had better be back to pick me up on the day I told them or they'll be in for real trouble.'

Bill Brighty kept very quiet

because he didn't know whether the crew of the *Crooked Crab* meant to come back for Captain McCorkell at all.

Then he sneezed six times and the Captain took him up to the shop to see if they could get him something better in the way of clothes. After the plank and his swim in the sea and the long row, he looked rather the worse for wear.

When the lady in the shop saw

Bill Brighty, she cried, 'You poor, poor man. Come in to the back and warm yourself and I'll give you something for that dreadful cold.'

And she took him off and made him sit with his feet in a hot bath. Then she tucked him up in bed in her spare bedroom and fed him on lovely nourishing food.

Captain McCorkell was no better off for company after all and went back to mooching about on the beach by himself.

'A pretty poor do too,' he grumbled and spent the next few days scanning the horizon for sight of the *Crooked Crab*.

Chapter 6

When the crew found the hole in the
Crooked Crab, they plugged it
quickly as best they could. Then
they tried to get rid of the oil.

But they couldn't. It was in their
hair and in their shoes.

The chocolate mousse tasted of it

and so did the grog and it cured them all of ever wanting either again.

The engine had never had so much oil in all its life and it refused to start. So Bracken had to mend the mast and they managed to put up a sail of sorts and they limped along with a following breeze at a very slow rate of knots.

The question was, where should they go?

Now they all realised that the only man who could ever get the *Crooked Crab* shipshape again was Captain McCorkell. And despite the fact that they knew they were in for the most terrible trouble, after several hours of argument even Potter agreed that they had better return to the island and collect the Captain. If they kept going as they were, they would just about get back on the right day.

So it came about that, on the very Saturday they were expected, the *Crooked Crab* stole into the bay opposite the house where the Captain was staying and quietly dropped anchor. And because they had no tub to row to the beach, the crew had to wait until the Captain came out to them.

It is better left unwritten what Captain McCorkell said to the crew of the *Crooked Crab*. But for the next few days the four sailors (for Bill Brighty didn't lift a finger to help) worked as they had never worked before and the quantities of hot water and the scrubbing and the polishing and painting had to be

seen to be believed. Captain
McCorkell took less than a minute
to get back to his roaring and
managing and was pleased as could
be that his holiday was over for
another fifteen years. And the crew
were so glad to get things straight
that no question of mutiny ever
crossed their minds again.

The only change was in the mate,
Bill Brighty.

Bill Brighty had decided that he
had had enough of the sea and the
crew of the *Crooked Crab*. He
thought that he would far rather
spend the next few years saying
"yes" to the shop lady than to
Captain McCorkell. He liked
counting up the money in her till

each evening and gathering her apples and sometimes milking her cow. His cold had nearly gone and the shop lady said he was really useful and could stay as long as he pleased.

So when Captain McCorkell sang out 'All aboard' on the morning of the *Crooked Crab's* departure, for the first and last time Bill Brighty said "no". And he stayed on the island.

And after all that seemed to suit everyone.

So once again the *Crooked Crab* sailed out to sea with her

grumbling, grousing crew. But things weren't quite the same. She had a patch on her side as well as on her sail—and she hadn't got a mate.

And if anyone mentioned the

words "oil" or "chocolate mousse"
the whole crew turned green and
refused to speak. As for Potter the
Cook, never again was he heard to
fry his aunty. He might boil her or
bake her—but he never fried her . . .

MIDNIGHT PIRATE

BY DIANA HENDRY
ILLUSTRATED BY JANET DUCHESNE

'Oh Pirate, dear little Pirate,' whispered Ida, 'you can't stay here. The Aunts don't want a kitten.'

Nothing Ida could say would make the Aunts change their minds and it seemed as though the tiny kitten she had found under the holly bush would have to stay out in the cold and wet, unloved by anyone.

But the kitten had other ideas and even the Aunts became involved in what happened next . . .

0 552 524174

URSULA CAMPING

BY SHEILA LAVELLE
ILLUSTRATED BY THELMA LAMBERT

Ursula is an ordinary girl — with one special
difference. If she eats a currant bun, stuffed with a
mixture of porridge oats and honey, and recites a
magic spell, she can turn herself into a real, live, little
bear!

When she runs up against trouble from her two
cousins, Ian and Jamie, while on a camping holiday in
the New Forest, Ursula finds that being able to
change herself into a bear can be very useful
indeed . . .

0 552 524476

60

THE HAUNTING OF HEMLOCK HALL

BY LANCE SALWAY
ILLUSTRATED BY CATHIE SHUTTLEWORTH

'There's no ghosts at Hemlock Hall. Never have been and never will,' the old gardener tells Tom when he comes to work there in the holidays.

But the awful new owners, the Trotters, have other ideas. When they open the Hall to the public, they are determined that ghosts shall be among its many attractions . . .

0 552 524166

MY GANG

BY CATHERINE SEFTON
ILLUSTRATED BY CATHERINE BRADBURY

'This is my gang, Noel!' said Marty. 'It's girls only, and we're tough. We'll wallop you if you start mucking things up! Right, gang?'

Being looked after by his big sister and her gang is no joke for Noel, especially as they won't let him join. But soon Noel finds a way of making sure that he is not the only one left out . . .

0 552 524158

THE KILLER TADPOLE

BY JACQUELINE WILSON
ILLUSTRATED BY LESLEY SMITH

'Do you want to be in my gang?' Spike hissed.

Well, Spike was very good at bashing people up, so how could Nicholas refuse? But, to join the gang, he has to undergo three Terrible Ordeals.

To Nicholas's amazement, one of the Ordeals ends with a big surprise — a tadpole that keeps growing, and growing, and growing until it becomes what must be the largest tadpole in the world — the Killer Tadpole! Perhaps it can save him from Spike — and from getting bashed up!

0 552 52414X

If you would like to receive a Newsletter about our new Children's books, just fill in the coupon below with your name and address (or copy it onto a separate piece of paper if you don't want to spoil your book) and send it to:

The Children's Books Editor
Young Corgi Books
61-63 Uxbridge Road,
Ealing
London W5 5SA

Please send me a Children's Newsletter:

Name . . . .

Address . . . .

. . . .

. . . .

All the books on the previous pages are available at your local bookshop or can be ordered direct from the publishers: Cash Sales Dept., Transworld Publishers Ltd., 61-63 Uxbridge Road, Ealing, London W5 5SA.

Please enclose the cost of the book(s), together with the following for postage and packing costs:

Orders up to a value of £5.00	50p
Orders of a value over £5.00	Free

Please note that payment should be made by cheque or postal order in £ sterling.